ESCAPE FROM...

the Terrorist Attacks of 9/11

This is a work of fiction. Any references to historical events, real people, or real places are used fictitiously. Other names, characters, places, and events are products of the author's imagination, and any resemblance to actual events or places or persons, living or dead, is entirely coincidental.

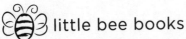 little bee books

New York, NY
Copyright © 2021 by Little Bee Books
All rights reserved, including the right of reproduction
in whole or in part in any form.
Manufactured in the United States of America LSC 0621
First Edition
10 9 8 7 6 5 4 3 2 1
Library of Congress Cataloging-in-Publication Data
is available upon request.
ISBN 978-1-4998-1169-8
littlebeebooks.com
For information about special discounts on bulk purchases, please
contact Little Bee Books at sales@littlebeebooks.com.

ESCAPE FROM...

the Terrorist Attacks of 9/11

by Elaine Berkowitz

illustrated by Shen Fei

little bee books

PROLOGUE

September 11, 2001, 8:14 AM

The passengers of American Airlines Flight 11 settle into their narrow seats, just fifteen minutes into a six-hour flight. They have taken off on time from Boston's Logan Airport this beautiful Tuesday morning, and are headed across the country to Los Angeles, California.

The eleven crew members have worked this route many times. The weather is clear. It should be a smooth, ordinary flight. But five passengers on board know differently. They have a plan, one they have been plotting for many months. And they are prepared to carry it out no matter what.

The cabin is dim. The only sound is from the wind

rushing outside the windows. But the calm is broken by sudden movement at the front of the plane. Five men have gotten out of their seats. They are rushing toward the cockpit. Sensing trouble, a number of passengers and flight attendants try to hold the men back. But though they are outnumbered, these men have weapons. Screams ring out as three people are stabbed.

"Nobody move!" one of the men yells. "If you try anything, you'll endanger yourself. Just stay quiet."

Word spreads quickly through the plane. The flight has been hijacked!

Sixteen minutes after Flight 11's takeoff, another plane, United Airlines Flight 175, departs from Logan Airport, also bound for Los Angeles. About thirty minutes into the flight, five men get up. Two of the men force their way into the cockpit, where the pilot is flying the plane. The other three men push all the passengers to the back. Panicked travelers cry out in fear and worry. The aircraft is being flown so poorly that they just miss crashing into two other planes in the sky. Plus, the plane is dipping lower and lower. It is clear to everyone on board that they are in serious danger.

Elsewhere, similar events are unfolding aboard two other aircraft. These four flights have a few key things in common. They all take off from the East Coast and are headed to the West Coast. All four aircraft are large and have tanks filled with thousands of gallons of fuel to fly the long distance. These planes are traveling at about 500 miles per hour. They are dangerous weapons, and they are in the wrong hands.

Together, nineteen men hijack four planes this morning. It is a carefully planned effort to harm as many people as possible. America is under attack.

REALITY CHECK:

How could nineteen terrorists get through airport security without any of them being stopped?

On September 11, 2001, all the hijackers passed through security without a problem. Some of the men *were* stopped when they set off metal detectors. But after brief inspections, they were allowed through. Before 9/11, airport security was much different than it is today. Back then, you could bring a baseball bat, scissors, and even a box cutter on board a plane. In fact, blades smaller than four inches long were considered okay, too! Security only looked for obvious weapons, like guns and bombs.

The events of 9/11 forever changed the way airport security is conducted. Now, the United States maintains a "do not fly" list, where any person suspected of being involved in terrorism is not allowed through security. Airports also have more advanced screening procedures. Body scanners, for example, detect not only metal, but any hidden item that could potentially be used as a weapon.

Security aboard planes themselves also changed after 9/11. It is required that airlines secure cockpit doors. By making them stronger, it is less likely that a hijacking could happen.

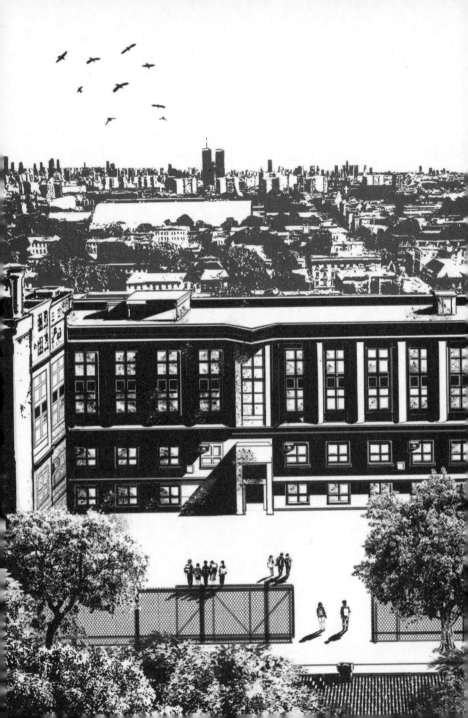

CHAPTER 1

TONY

September 11, 2001, 7:45 AM

"Everyone, look this way. Pay attention!" Ms. Monroe claps her hands together loudly and speaks in her serious voice. "EVERYONE!" she bellows. I look up from my comic book and squint in the bright morning light. Around me, the other kids in Ms. Monroe's sixth-grade class are spread out on the school steps. The group is bouncing with energy. It's the first class trip of the year!

The chatting dies down as everyone turns their attention to Ms. Monroe.

"Okay, let's discuss some rules. First, and most importantly," she yells with her pointer finger held high, "you must pay attention and stay with the group. If you need something, don't be shy. Just speak up."

She gestures to a young teacher in jeans and a plaid button-down standing off to the side. "We also have Mr. Thompson with us today. He's here to help make sure we get every single one of you to the city and back. Do not make me have to explain to your parents how we lost one of their children on our first trip!"

At that, a few kids giggle, but Ms. Monroe quickly cuts them off. "I will be paying close attention to your behavior today, and you DO NOT want to disappoint me."

Ms. Monroe means business! It's only the second week of school and we're all still getting to know each other. So far, the teachers at Brooklyn's Middle School 88 have been pretty easygoing. They let us choose our own seats in electives, and they don't seem to mind too much when someone needs to borrow a pencil or forgets a book. Ms. Monroe even brought us homemade chocolate chip cookies last Friday to celebrate a successful first week. So far, I'm liking middle school.

I look around at the group of kids. I know some from elementary school, but there are still a lot of new faces for me. Leon and Chloe P. have been in my class the last four years. Emerson, Jake, and Ayelet were in my fifth-grade class last year. Since it's only the first week of school, everyone is sticking with people they already know. But I don't want to hang out with the same people I always have. I'm curious about the other kids. Yesterday, I overheard Asim talking about how to draw Bart Simpson. And Rick is always carrying a Series of Unfortunate Events book with him. There are finally kids in my class that like the same stuff I do! Now, I just have to find out how to be friends with them.

Ms. Monroe interrupts my thoughts with one last announcement. "We're going to be walking down Union Street to Fourth Avenue to catch an N or an R train into the city. Does everyone have their paper?"

I feel for the folded-up newspaper in my back pocket. We were all given the business section of the newspaper to use in a lesson about the stock exchange. A chorus of "yes" and "yep" rings out and finally, we're ready to go.

As we start down the street in messy rows of twos and threes, I feel my stomach flip-flop. Just one week ago, it had seemed like a great idea to invite the class to visit my dad's office in Manhattan. Dad is a financial advisor at Morgan Stanley. His job is to help people manage their money. Scanning the *Wall Street Journal*'s stock tables over cereal has been our breakfast ritual for years. So when I told Dad that our class would be learning about the stock market in social studies, he nearly choked on his Corn Flakes. This was one subject he's an expert in!

Dad put down his spoon and looked at me excitedly. He asked, "Do you think your class would want to visit my office?"

"I think so!" I said with a smile.

"Great!" he practically shouted.

When I ask Ms. Monroe, she seems equally as excited for the class to visit Morgan Stanley. In all her years teaching social studies, this would be the first time she took a class trip to Manhattan's World Trade Center. I just hope it will be at least a little interesting. I will be so embarrassed if it turns out to be boring.

REALITY CHECK:

WAS THERE ANY WARNING OR INDICATION THAT THE U.S. WOULD BE UNDER ATTACK THAT DAY?

There was no specific threat to the U.S. on that particular day, but over the previous few years, the country had become concerned about a terrorist group in the Middle East called al Qaeda. Terrorists are people that use violence to spread their message. Osama bin Laden was the founder and leader of al Qaeda. The U.S. government, as well of those of other countries, knew he posed a risk, but they did not know he had planned to use planes as weapons against the U.S.

CHAPTER 2

ELIZABETH

September 11, 2001, 7:55 AM

I can't take my eyes off the cloudless blue sky. It's as bright as the aquamarine ring Grandma Mimi always wears. For as long as I can remember, my grandma never leaves the house without her silver ring with a bright blue stone. Aquamarine is the color of the ocean. She wears the ring, she says, because it makes her feel at peace, like she is when she's at the beach. I try it on whenever I can, so I can feel like I am at the beach, too. Grandma Mimi promised that one day the ring would be mine.

Grandma Mimi walks me to my new school. As we stroll, I list all the things in my head I miss about my

13

old neighborhood. Our apartment had a small courtyard where all the building kids would play after school. And there was a grocery store on the corner that sold frozen ice pops for a quarter. I even miss the sweet old men playing chess in the park. I've known them my whole life.

Since the start of the school year, I have tried talking to new people. But I don't always know what to say. Some of these kids have gone to school together their whole lives! No one else seems to be looking for a new friend.

At my old school in Queens, I had lots of friends. I still talk to them on the phone and visit sometimes. But I know the year will be long and lonely if I don't connect with anyone here. Brooklyn is right next to Queens, so why does it feel like a whole other world?

As always, Grandma Mimi knows just what to say. "Elizabeth, my love. Everything will work out. Give it time."

I sigh. "It's already been a week!" I say.

14

Grandma Mimi laughs and bends down so we are eye to eye. "It's hard to make friends at a new school. I totally understand. But you haven't given anyone a chance to get to know you yet! You are someone very special. Any of those kids would be lucky to count you as a friend. Never forget that."

I give her a tiny smile. I hope my grandmother is right.

We stop at the entrance to Middle School 88. With a wink, Grandma Mimi slips a five-dollar bill into my hand. I thank her and wish her a great day.

Only an hour later, I am admiring the color of the sky and remembering my grandmother's words. I get swept up by the group of kids walking down Union Street. We are headed to the subway for the first school trip of the year. Two girls just in front of me are laughing about something they saw on TV. Are they talking about a show I have watched? Or a movie? I try to listen over the sounds of the New York City morning. Following the girls closely, I step off the curb into the street before a hard tug on my arm pulls me backward. At the same time, my ears fill with the loud squeal of tires. A horn honks and the driver yells, "Hey! Watch where you're going!"

I can feel the blood rush to my cheeks. The whole class stops and looks right at me. I am frozen in place! The boy who had grabbed my arm comes to my side. "Are you okay?" he asks. I manage to nod my head, but I fight back tears. Inside, I wish more than ever that I had a friend.

REALITY CHECK:

DID SCHOOLS HAVE TRIPS ON 9/11?

The week of September 11, 2001, was only the second week of school in New York City. It's not likely that any of the schools scheduled class trips that day.

In Washington, DC, three schoolkids and three teachers got on a plane that morning. They had been chosen for a special trip to study ecology in California. The students, Asia Cottom, Bernard Brown, and Rodney Dickens, were all just eleven years old. They were traveling with their teachers, Hilda Taylor, James Debeuneure, and Sara Clark. Sadly, their plane was the third to be hijacked that day. When it crashed into the Pentagon, everyone on board was killed.

The victims are remembered today at the Pentagon Memorial. There, a bench sits for each lost life. Every year on the anniversary of 9/11, families and friends gather there to remember their lost loved ones.

CHAPTER 3

TONY

September 11, 2001, 8:05 AM

The walk to the train is helping to settle my nerves. Jake and I are talking about the U.S. Open matches we caught on TV this past weekend. Five days earlier, a match between Pete Sampras and Andre Agassi lasted three and a half hours! I had never seen anything like it.

"I didn't want to miss a minute of it," I tell Jake. "By the end of the match, I had to pee so badly!"

He laughs and nods his head. "It was so close the whole time!"

"Man, I would give anything to be able to play like Agassi," I say. "Did you play a lot and get much better at camp?"

Jake had spent a week upstate at tennis camp this past summer. "Yeah, I got better. But not like, *Agassi* better!" he laughs.

"What kind of stuff did you do?" I ask.

"We did a lot of drills. I worked on my serve a bunch. The coaches really kept us moving all day. All that running around made me so hungry! And then they would serve the weirdest food. Like this veggie loaf," he explains, crinkling his nose. "It was brown and soft and just wrong! *Blech*."

"Stop, I'm gonna barf!" I tell him.

We're laughing so hard, it takes us by surprise when a girl in front of us steps off the sidewalk and right into traffic! I reach out and grab her arm, pulling her back just in time. A moment later and she could have been hit by that car!

I ask if she is alright. She isn't hurt, but she does seem a little startled. I try to laugh it off so she doesn't feel bad. "Don't worry," I say with a warm smile. "It happens to the best of us."

She manages a small laugh, but I can tell she's still feeling weird about it.

"Hey, I'm Tony," I say. "I don't think we've met yet."

"Yeah, I don't think so," she replies. "I'm Elizabeth. And I swear, I do know how to cross a street!"

We both laugh and the tension starts to fade.

When the light changes, Elizabeth, Jake, and I all cross the street together and rejoin the rest of the class. Ms. Monroe and Mr. Thompson are standing at the entrance to the subway station.

Ms. Monroe waits until we are all together and addresses the group. "Okay!" she says. "Now everyone, please remember the most important thing is to pay attention and stick together. It's rush hour, so it may be very crowded. Just please stay with the class."

Ms. Monroe waves us down a set of stairs. At the bottom, Mr. Thompson swipes each of us through a turnstile with a MetroCard. Once our fares are paid, we head down another set of steps to wait for the Manhattan-bound train.

We walk single file down the long platform to find a place to stand together. I notice the many different types of people standing nearby. Young people, probably on their way to school. Men and women on their way to work. One guy is as old as my great-grandfather. I wonder where my dad stands when he waits in this station every morning on his way to work.

"You're wrong, man. *The Empire Strikes Back* is the best. I have one word for you . . . YODA!" Jake and Asim are arguing about which of the original Star Wars trilogy movies is better. The teachers are discussing a book they had both read. The sounds of chatter all around us gives way to a loud rumbling. With a shriek of wheels hitting the tracks, our train pulls into the station.

The doors swoosh open. We stand to the side to let people off. Ms. Monroe waits until the whole class is on, then squeezes in behind us. I find myself wedged between Mr. Thompson and an older man in a suit trying to read the paper. My face is inches away from it with nowhere else to look. On the page, a woman's face is lit from the glow of a computer screen. I read, "Tonight, she won't scramble for the IT guy's pager number."

It's an ad for some new computer software that saves work automatically. I remember the English paper I lost last year when the power went out during a storm. I had to stay up until midnight to rewrite the whole thing. That software would have sure come in handy then!

After a few stops, the older man shuffles his newspaper, and now I'm face-to-face with the TV listings. I study the morning and afternoon schedules. If I were home right now, would I be watching *The Today Show* or *Good Morning America*? I scan the evening listings and try to guess what we'll watch tonight after dinner. Dad and I like to catch *The Simpsons*, but Mom always wants to watch *Friends*. Sometimes, if I've finished my homework and gotten ready for bed without arguing, my dad lets me stay up a little late to watch *Frasier*. It's not even that funny, but I love being up past my bedtime.

My thoughts are interrupted by the crackle of the

subway speaker. In a booming voice, the conductor announces: "Next stop, Cortlandt Street."

We'll reach our stop in a couple of minutes. I think about all the ways today could go horribly wrong. As we pull into the station, something in my stomach is fluttering. We're finally here.

REALITY CHECK:

*WHAT'S A PAGER? WHY WOULDN'T THE
WOMAN IN THE AD JUST CALL THE IT GUY'S CELL PHONE?*

Before cellular phones were common, some people had a device called a "pager" (also known as a "beeper"). It's a small, wireless gadget that can receive messages. This is how they work: If you want to get in touch with someone who has a pager, you would use the keypad on a phone to send a message to it. The pager would beep to let the owner know they had a message. (That's why it's called a "beeper"!)

Pagers themselves cannot make calls or send messages. So if a person receives a message on their pager, they can't respond. One benefit of a pager is that they are very reliable. They don't lose service like cell phones do. And their batteries last for weeks before needing to be charged.

In 2001, many people did have cell phones. But pagers were still in use. Even today, you might occasionally see a doctor or firefighter using a pager. They're still a very reliable way to receive messages.

CHAPTER 4

ELIZABETH

September 11, 2001, 8:20 AM

I am trying to stay close to my teacher as we walk along Church Street. Even though the subway has taken us across the East River and we are only a few miles from school, Manhattan feels like another world to me. Tall buildings sprout from the ground and loom high above us. The sidewalks buzz with people. I feel the energy of the city like a force bringing me to life. The cars honking, the smell of coffee and street-vendor pretzels, the blur of people—I want to hold onto this feeling and never let it go.

Ms. Monroe stops in front of a huge black building that takes up the entire block. "I wanted to show you this building. This is One Liberty Street. It used to be called the U.S. Steel Building. Can anyone guess why?"

Ayelet, one of the girls I listened in on earlier, is quick to answer. "Because it's made of steel?"

Ms. Monroe smiles. She replies, "Yes! But it was also built for the U.S. Steel Company. That was back in 1972. But there's an even more interesting history here. The Singer Building was built in 1908. At that time, it was the tallest building ever built! But a year later, an even taller building was constructed!"

Ms. Monroe keeps talking, but I am distracted. I am thinking about the tallest building I have ever been to. Last year, my class took a trip to visit the Willamsburgh Savings Bank Tower in Brooklyn. We were all excited because our teacher said we could choose our seatmate for the bus ride. I wanted to sit with a friend, but I didn't know which one to choose. Phoebe had been my best friend since second grade when we discovered we both collected Beanie Babies. We could play with those stuffed animals for hours! My favorite was Patti the platypus and Phoebe's was a cow named Daisy. It's no wonder our teachers called us Frick and Frack.

By the start of fifth grade, Rosie and I had bonded over our love of *The Powerpuff Girls*. Sometimes after school, Rosie would come to my apartment and we'd watch it for hours.

Choosing between Phoebe and Rosie gave me a stomachache. I didn't know what to do! So when the new girl, Ella, needed someone to sit with, I was quick to volunteer.

At first, Phoebe and Rosie were mad. But I told them, "I couldn't choose between you!" Also, I had a great idea to keep them from being annoyed with me. "I think you two should sit together on the bus!" I suggested.

When we arrived at the old bank building, we were given a tour of the old banking hall. It was unlike anything I had ever seen. Overhead, the tall ceiling was painted to look like the night sky. The floor was a colorful marble puzzle. A huge mural of Henry Hudson's ship decorated one wall. We learned that for many years, this thirty-seven-story building was the tallest in Brooklyn. We also learned that day that Phoebe, Rosie, and Ella had a lot in common!

I snap back to Ms. Monroe. She had moved on to something else and is now pointing out buildings across the street. She motions to two impossibly tall skyscrapers that seem to reach the clouds.

Ms. Monroe explains, "These were built in 1970. At the time, they beat out the Empire State Building for tallest in the world." We all tip our heads back as far as they can go to see to the tops of them.

They seem so much taller than anything I had ever seen! "Ms. Monroe?" I ask. "How many stories are they?"

My teacher's eyes grow wide as she answers, "A hundred and ten stories each!" That is almost three times taller than the tallest building I had ever been in! I wish Phoebe, Rosie, and Ella were here with me now. Next to the Twin Towers, I feel especially small and alone.

REALITY CHECK:

WAS THE WORLD TRADE CENTER REALLY THAT BIG?

Yes! The World Trade Center was so big that it needed its own zip code! The seven buildings that made up the World Trade Center complex took up sixteen acres of land. Many of the buildings were used for office space. There was also an underground shopping mall and a hotel. In the center of the buildings, a five-acre plaza held concerts and other events.

The Twin Towers themselves were enormous. Each floor was about an acre in size. That means that each floor was about the size of a football field. And with 110 stories in each tower, that's like 220 football fields stacked on top of one another! A massive amount of material was used to construct the towers. Workers put in over 40,000 doors and 43,000 windows. If you laid out all the electrical wiring that was used, it would be over 3,000 miles long.

CHAPTER 5

TONY

September 11, 2001, 8:30 AM

As we enter the lobby of 2 World Trade Center, our eyes go wide with wonder. Light floods in from the walls of windows around us. So many men and women streaming in, heading to work. Ms. Monroe gathers everyone off to the side to keep us out of the way.

"Okay, everyone! We made it. Stay put for a moment while I call up to our host," she says with a nod in my direction. I feel heat prickle my cheeks. I wonder if I have maybe made a terrible mistake. But then I remember how excited my dad got when he heard we were learning about the stock market. How could I have said no?

Ms. Monroe approaches the security desk with a bright "Good morning!" As she chatters to the desk staff, Asim elbows me lightly in the ribs. Smiling, he asks, "So what's the deal? What's your dad gonna show us?" A few other kids look up, curious to hear what we'll be doing.

I have no idea. My dad hasn't told me anything! I shrug and say, "I have no clue. I don't know if he planned something special or we're just getting a tour. . . ." I trail off, hoping that will end the conversation.

Chloe P. is standing at the edge of the group slowly turning in all directions to take it all in. She pipes up from the side, "Tony, where do those escalators go?" She points to a row of escalators nearby.

I shrug. "No clue," I mumble. I look over to see if Ms. Monroe is coming back. She is still talking to one of the building's workers, who has a phone pressed to his ear. He says something that makes her laugh. I wish they would hurry up.

Ayelet asks me about the elevators. "There must be

like a million," she says. "Do you know how many there are?" I just shrug. I stuff my hands in my jeans pockets and look down at my sneakers.

Elizabeth, who has been quietly watching me get more and more uncomfortable, also has a question. She clears her throat and quietly asks, "Um, Tony?" I look up at her but she can't read my eyes. She asks, "Do you know how long your dad has worked here?"

I let out a breath I didn't know I was holding. I stammer, "Uh, yeah. Yes! I do know that. I was little, so I don't really remember it," I start. "But I know it was his first week working here. And a bomb went off."

That gets everyone's attention. Even Asim, who has been hopping from one foot to another, stops hopping. "A *real* bomb?" he asks.

Mr. Thompson pipes up. "That's right, I remember that," he says. "What was that, 1993, 1994?"

"It was 1993," I say. "Someone put a bomb in a truck and parked it in a garage under the building. My dad was away from the building at lunch when it happened.

35

And when he got back, all these people were standing outside. Firefighters, police, emergency workers. He said the towers were full of smoke. And one of his coworkers got stuck in an elevator for five hours."

"Five hours!" Asim yells. "What if he had to poop!?"

Everyone bursts out laughing, and Mr. Thompson's face turns serious. "Asim," he says really slowly, but Asim keeps talking.

"But I'm serious, Mr. Thompson. That's a long time. What if he had prunes for breakfast? What if he had cheese with lunch?"

Mr. Thompson barely contains a laugh. "Cheese, Asim?"

Asim shrugs. "I'm lactose-intolerant, okay?"

Elizabeth isn't distracted by Asim's silliness. She's still thinking about the bombing. "That's so crazy. Was everyone alright?" she asks.

"I don't think so," I answer. "A few people died. And I know a lot of people were hurt. Dad said people were scared to come back to work here even after everything was fixed."

Ms. Monroe is finally heading back from the front desk. She catches the tail end of what I am saying. "Scared to go back to what?" she asks.

Before anyone can answer, Jake spots my dad walking toward us. With a wave, he calls, "Hey, Mr. Bauer!"

My stomach starts to feel funny again. But when I turn and see my dad's huge smile, I start to relax. Maybe today won't be so bad.

REALITY CHECK:

WAS THERE A BOMBING AT THE WORLD TRADE CENTER IN 1993?
Yes, there really was an attack at the World Trade Center in 1993. On February 26, two men drove a rented van into a parking garage underneath the World Trade Center. The van held a 1,200-pound bomb.

When the bomb went off, the explosion rocked the North Tower. Power to the elevators and sprinklers and much of the electricity went down. It blew a 100-foot-wide hole in the building. It took rescue workers over five hours to get everyone out of the building.

At the time, it was the deadliest terrorist attack to happen on U.S soil. Six people lost their lives and about 1,000 were injured. All but one of the seven men that planned and carried out the attack were caught. They were found guilty and went to jail for the rest of their lives.

CHAPTER 6

ELIZABETH

September 11, 2001, 8:35 AM

When I see Mr. Bauer, I can't help but smile. He is walking so fast through the lobby, he is almost jogging. I can feel his excitement. He waves at us with both hands as he gets near. "Hello, hello!" he says. "I'm so glad you made it. How was the train ride?"

Ms. Monroe steps forward and introduces herself. "Thank you so much for having us today. As we learn more about the stock market, it'll be so helpful to have input from an expert."

"My pleasure," he replies. "Glad to have you. I feel honored that you're visiting me on your first school trip. We're going to be heading up to the Morgan

Stanley office on the seventy-fourth floor. Follow me!"

As we walk, he looks at Tony and jokes, "Do I know you? You look familiar."

I laugh. Ms. Monroe does, too. "I can tell we're going to have a great time today," she says.

We walk past security and over to a shiny bank of elevators. As we wait, Mr. Bauer starts to tell us a story. "When I was about your age," he begins, "I read the Sunday paper with my gramps every week. I'd grab the comics. He'd grab the classifieds. When I saw something especially funny, I'd show him."

Tony interrupts, "And let me guess. When he saw a boat he wanted, he'd show you?"

"How did you know?" Mr. Bauer laughs. "Sorry, kid. I know you've heard this story before."

"Like a hundred times!" Tony says with a chuckle.

"Like a hundred times," he admits. "I'll do the short version." He clears his throat and continues. "Like I was saying, Gramps and I had a tradition. Well, one Sunday, the paper didn't show up. Up and down the street, no one got their paper. We didn't know what to do with ourselves. So, Gramps has the brilliant idea to go find last week's paper."

An elevator dings. He motions for everyone to get on as he holds the door open.

He continues. "So, he looks all over the house—upstairs, downstairs—and finally finds it. But all that was left was the Business and Finance section. My mom used the rest of it to line the cat's litter box."

We all manage to fit in one elevator. Mr. Bauer presses the button for 74 and the doors close. He continues, "With no other options, we ended up looking through it together. That day, he taught me how to read the stock tables. And from then on, we read them every Sunday. In addition to the comics and the classifieds, of course."

As the elevator climbs, my head starts to feel funny. The lit-up numbers above the doors are moving too quickly. Floors 6, 7, 8 go by in an instant. I close my eyes, waiting for the feeling to pass.

Mr. Bauer continues his story. "Every year on my

birthday, instead of giving me toys, Gramps gave me stocks. And every Sunday, we'd see how my stocks were doing," he tells us. "I used to joke that I would buy him a boat one day."

I am not the only one noticing how fast we are moving. Chloe P. points to the glowing numbers on the wall and says, "Woah, we're flying."

"Feels like it! These elevators go 1,600 feet per minute. The building is just over 1,300 feet tall. So give or take, they can take you from the lobby to the top floor in one minute," he tells us. "There are 110 floors. But we're only going to 74."

I feel like my stomach has dropped to my knees. I hope no one notices that my face has started to sweat. I try to keep my breathing steady. When Tony sees I have pressed my eyes closed, he leans over and whispers, "Don't worry. We're almost there."

I can't stop thinking about the man that was trapped in the elevator for five hours. If we get stuck, there won't be enough room for people to sit down. There won't be enough oxygen to breathe! Or worse, what if the cable snaps? What if we free-fall from seventy-four stories up? I feel dizzy and it's getting worse by the second.

REALITY CHECK:

HOW MANY PEOPLE PASSED THROUGH THE WORLD TRADE CENTER ON AN AVERAGE WEEKDAY?

The World Trade Center complex was a group of seven buildings that sat together in Lower Manhattan. The two, 110-foot-tall towers that sat in the center were known as the Twin Towers. They were the tallest buildings in all of New York City. Each stood about 1,400 feet high. More than 400 companies had offices at the World Trade Center. The buildings had enough office space to hold 35,000 workers. Many thousands of tourists also visited each day. It's estimated that on an average weekday, 70,000 people passed through the complex.

When al Qaeda planned the attack on the United States, they chose the Twin Towers for two reasons. One was that it was the financial center of the country. But it was also chosen because of the potential to hurt as many people as possible.

45

CHAPTER 7

TONY

September 11, 2001, 8:40 AM

As we ride the elevator to my dad's office, I see Elizabeth is looking a little pale. I'm not feeling quite like myself today, either. I've bitten my nails down to tiny nubs.

Ms. Monroe herds us off the elevator and into a small waiting area. As we cross the room, she reminds everyone, "I expect each and every one of you to be on your best behavior. This is a place of business. Please be respectful."

My dad uses a key card to open a nearby door. We follow him down an aisle beside rows of cubicles. It is early, so not many people have come to work yet. The office is quiet. The class manages to keep the volume down to a low murmur. That is, until Chloe P. catches sight of the view. "Holy moly!" she yells.

We pause to see what has gotten Chloe's attention. Beyond the cubicles, there are offices with walls of windows. Looking out, it feels like we are seeing the entire city. A hush comes over us as we take it all in. From up here, the buildings look like stacked Legos, pieced together with different-size bricks. You can see the edge of the island, then water. I have seen this view before, but never on a day like today. The sky is so clear, a vast blue stretching on forever.

"Wow. That is really something," says Ms. Monroe.

"Never gets old," I reply.

Jake points beyond the water, to some land on the other side. He asks, "Mr. Bauer, what's over there?"

"Oh, that is a great question," he says. "Does anyone know what's over there across the water?"

When no one answers, my dad says, "New Jersey!"

But he says it with a silly accent so it sounds like New *Joisey*. Some kids laugh. I silently wish I could melt into the carpet.

We continue walking. We turn into a conference room with folding chairs set up in neat rows.

My dad flicks on the lights. "Come on in," he says. "Grab a seat. Get comfortable."

I grab a seat in the back row. Asim sits down next to me. The other seats fill up around us.

Once everyone is settled, my dad begins talking. "I'm really excited to have you here today. Before we start, I need to ask you all a very important question." He pauses to get everyone's attention. "Do you like money? Raise your hand if you do."

Everyone's hands shoot up. "Okay," he continues. "You all like money. Well, money plays a big role in my job as a financial planner. I help people make and manage their money. And one tool that helps me do that is the stock market. Today, I will share with you how I do that." He smiles at the group. "Did everyone bring the stock tables?"

There are murmurs of "yes" as we all pull out our newspapers.

I open my mouth to ask Asim a question, but the sound of a loud *BOOM!* cuts me off.

I sit up straight. The sound is like a single firework. It is followed by a rumble that is unlike anything I have felt before. I can see a slight change in my dad's expression. Is he . . . worried?

At once, kids are chattering. Everyone seems to be asking the same question: "What was that?"

With a wrinkled forehead, my dad puts down his newspaper. "Hang on a sec," he says. "Let me check that out. I'll be right back."

As my dad heads for the conference room door, I stand up. Through the open doorway, I can see a few people standing in their cubicles. Someone I can't see is screaming, but I don't understand what they're saying. Everyone's eyes are fixed in the same direction. Dad turns to see what they are all staring at. His eyes go wide and he raises his hand to cover his open mouth. My heart starts hammering in my chest. I know something is really wrong.

REALITY CHECK:

COULD THE PEOPLE IN 2 WORLD TRADE CENTER ACTUALLY FEEL WHAT HAPPENED AT 1 WORLD TRADE CENTER?

We know from eyewitness accounts that people in the South Tower (#2) heard and felt a blast from the North Tower (#1). The towers were not that far apart—less than 200 feet. That's shorter than a city block. Also, the towers had walls of windows that looked out at the city. For those on the north side of 2 World Trade Center, there was no missing it. Both the loud booming sound and the force that rocked the buildings made it clear that something terrible had happened at 1 World Trade Center.

CHAPTER 8

ELIZABETH

September 11, 2001, 8:47 AM

I am sitting in the front of the room. When the door opens, I see right away that something is wrong. The office that had been so calm and quiet just minutes ago when we walked through it seems out of control now. A man yells, "Step back!" I can hear a woman crying. Before I even know what is happening, I know that it is really bad.

Ms. Monroe has jumped to her feet. "It's okay," she says. "Let's all stay calm and we'll figure out what's going on." She motions to Mr. Thompson to stay with us. She walks out of the room and turns to see what everyone is looking at. We can't see our teacher, but we hear her gasp. A cold shiver runs down my spine. I feel my heart beat faster and realize I've been holding my breath.

At that moment, I can't take it any longer. I have to know what's happening. I sprint from my seat. What I see out the window makes me question whether I am awake or still sleeping. *This can't be real,* I think.

My classmates have run out behind me. Someone asks, "What is happening?" Someone else is whimpering that they want to leave.

From the window, we have a perfect view of the other tower. A thick cloud of smoke pours out from a hole in the side of the building. In the air, we see floating bits of white. I step forward to get a closer look at what it is. It's paper. Some of it has burned edges. There is so much of it.

Ms. Monroe puts out her arms to block the crowd of students coming to see. "It's not safe by the window," she says. "Everyone, back up!"

I don't understand what's going on. So many things

are happening at once. I hear someone say something about a plane. Someone else is yelling that it was a bomb. Another person seems to be frozen, silently staring at the window. I watch as Mr. Bauer rushes to one of the desks and picks up the phone. I can't hear what he is saying over the noise of yelling and stomping feet that are getting louder as people race around. But after a minute, he runs back with some news.

"A plane flew into the North Tower," he explains. "They're saying it was an accident. Probably a small passenger plane."

He runs his hand through his hair. He looks over at his son and seems to make a decision. "It doesn't seem like we're in any danger," he says. "But to be safe, I want to get you all out of the building."

He motions to the teachers. "Start taking them toward the elevator. Make sure you keep everyone together. I'll bring up the rear."

My classmates and I hurry back the way we came, past the cubicles and into the waiting area. Someone presses the button for an elevator. Small groups have huddled together. I catch pieces of the conversations happening around me. Everyone is confused and scared. I feel those things, too, but have no one to share it with. I ball my hands into fists to stop them from shaking.

Tony and his dad are standing off to the side. With his hand on his son's shoulder, Mr. Bauer is talking quietly to Tony. I can't see Tony's face, but I have an idea of how he feels. I wish I were anywhere else but here. I am so confused. What is happening?

My mind goes to the pieces of paper. If paper could fall from the hole in the building, what about the people? And what about the passengers on the plane? The pilot?

The elevator is taking forever. The adults discuss whether they should take the stairs. At seventy-four floors up, it will take a long time to get down to the ground.

Before they can agree, an announcement comes over the PA. The system crackles to life. A man's voice can be heard through the speakers: "May I have your attention, please? Building two is secure. I repeat, building two is secure. The incident occurred in building one. You may go back to your desks."

I exhale. I feel relieved. I can see in my classmates' faces that they, too, feel better. Still, it's hard to shake the feeling that something is wrong. After all, there is a fire raging just outside the building. How do we know we are truly safe?

REALITY CHECK:

Was there really an announcement telling workers in the South Tower to stay put?

Yes. After 9/11, survivors reported that inside the South Tower, there were announcements over the PA system saying they were safe. People were told to stay put. How could such a big mistake be made?

No one knew yet that the plane crash was an attack. They thought it was an accident. They had no reason to think it would happen again. It seemed safer at the time to keep the thousands of workers inside the South Tower.

After the first plane hit, 1 World Trade Center was evacuated. Thousands of workers streamed out of the building. At the same time, firefighters went into the building to help people and put out the flames. Emergency medical workers were on the scene to give medical care to the injured. It was a messy scene.

CHAPTER 9

TONY

September 11, 2001, 8:58 AM

My heart rate starts to slow down. Whatever happened hasn't affected our building . . . yet. My dad leads the students and teachers back toward the conference room.

The group slows as we pass the windows once more. In the short time we were gone, the flames and smoke have gotten much worse. The smoke is thick, pouring out of the building like it's coming out of a massive chimney now. The flames are impossibly high.

I take a step closer to the window and am hit by a wall of heat like I've opened an oven door to check on baking cookies. I yelp and step right back. My dad is at my side in a flash. When he feels how hot it is, he shouts, "Everyone, stay back from the windows!"

Asim walks over in a daze. He hasn't said much since we left the conference room. He keeps his eyes on the rising smoke and asks, "If it's this hot all the way over here, how hot is it inside the other building? What about the people who are there?"

I open my mouth to say something, but nothing comes out. My stomach drops. We are all realizing the horrible truth about what we are seeing. It isn't just a fire. The building is burning, but that isn't the worst of it. It is burning hot inside that building. The smoke has to be overpowering. And there are lots of people still in there.

Across the way, small pieces of the building are falling. I watch them sail to the ground from so high up.

I feel my dad's hand on the back of my head. I look up and we lock eyes. With a soft voice I say, "Dad? I'm scared." As soon as the words are out, tears gather in my eyes and threaten to fall. I bury my face in my hands so no one can see.

With my face covered, I try the trick my mom taught me for when I am really upset. She told me, "Breathe in to the count of three. One, two, three. Then breathe out to the count of four. One, two, three, four."

When I open my eyes, my dad is looking at me with worry. I motion for him to come closer. Quietly, so I don't scare anyone, I tell him how I'm feeling. "Something doesn't feel right," I say. In that moment, my fear is suddenly replaced with purpose. I feel certain that we need to leave. "This isn't safe. We need to go, Dad, NOW!"

Dad walks away from me and huddles with the teachers. They all agree. We will take the stairs. It isn't the fastest way down, but it is the safest.

Ms. Monroe tells us the plan. She announces, "We're going to calmly form a line. Staying together, we will walk down to the street. It may take a while since we're on a high floor. But there's no need to rush. No need to panic."

I feel a little bit better. We just need to get downstairs. Then my dad and I can go home. Maybe there is a tennis match on TV to watch together. Maybe we can order dinner and tell Mom about our wild day.

We all enter the stairwell after Ms. Monroe. Starting at the 74th floor, we begin the long walk down. There are other people also taking the stairs. A man and a woman walking behind us are talking loudly.

"That building is going to come down. And I don't want to be here when it does," the woman says.

The man replies, "There's no way. These buildings were constructed to stay standing no matter what. They're made of steel!"

"Steel can melt," she says. "And the damage from the plane took out at least three floors. I'm telling you, I'm getting out of this neighborhood as fast as I can."

As we pass the 70th floor, we are stopped by a man with a bullhorn. "Go back!" he yells. "It's safer inside the building! This building is secure!"

And that's when we feel the jolt of another explosion.

REALITY CHECK:

How could there be any confusion about what caused the North Tower to catch fire?

The plane that crashed into 1 WTC had flown into the north side of the building. Since the plane had hit from the north, from certain parts of the South Tower, people could only see that there was a hole. They didn't have a view of the other, far side of the building that didn't face them. That's where the plane had entered. There was also so much thick smoke. Those factors made it hard to see exactly what had happened.

CHAPTER 10

ELIZABETH

September 11, 2001, 9:03 AM

A loud bang shakes the building. I grab onto a banister so I won't topple over. Above and below, people momentarily lose their footing. They're knocked down like bowling pins. Everyone is yelling with confusion and fear. It is noisy, which only adds to the feeling of total chaos.

Then there is a loud sound like a thump. At the same time, a wave of heat shoots down the stairwell from above. I scream as pieces of the ceiling come raining down. A large crack splits a nearby wall open. I can't believe what I am seeing. I don't know whether to stand still or run!

People are moving in all directions now. In the commotion, I've already lost sight of half my class. I don't want to be separated from them! That thought is squashed when a tall man knocks into me. I lose my balance and fall into the woman in front of me. It takes all my strength to stay upright. If I go down, I could be trampled!

The building begins to move. Slowly, we tilt to one side. I am sure we are about to crash to the ground. But then we just sway all the way to the other side. We are wobbling back and forth. I imagine that the building is one huge tree branch, swaying side to side in the wind.

From behind us, someone yells, "Go! Go!" We all start to move, slowly at first. It is hard to stay steady. The floors are slanted and the walls are crumbling in places. My classmates and I keep bumping into each other. I can see flames flashing behind some cracks in the walls.

Ms. Monroe has stopped on a landing to check that all of us kids in the class are alright. Her hair is sticking up on one side of her head and her clothes are messy.

She's looking all around trying to spot everyone. As we pass, she offers comforting words. "You're okay," she says. "You're doing great. Keep going!" She calls out for Mr. Thompson to wait at the bottom of the next set of stairs.

We travel down slowly. Lights flicker. The heavy smell of smoke hangs in the air. Right behind me, Rick keeps coughing. I turn to ask if he's alright, but I can tell he's not. His eyes are red and watery. He is crying, trying to suck in air between sobs.

"Hey," I say. "It's going to be okay. Smoke rises. We're going down. The air should clear up."

He nods but doesn't say anything.

"Let's stick together, okay?" I say.

I try to make sense of what is happening. Can it be an earthquake? Is that why everything is falling apart around us? I think about the explosion and the fire. The building shaking and the smoke. I remember looking out the window of the 74th floor. Through a hole in the side of the other tower, smoke and flames were shooting out.

Whatever happened to *that* building is now happening to *this* one. Unless it is a coincidence?

I think back to what I heard inside Mr. Bauer's office. I heard someone use the word "bomb." A million questions run through my mind. Has someone tried to blow up both buildings? What if it wasn't just these two buildings? Could the entire city be under attack? The whole country?

Or maybe it was just an accident? Maybe whatever it was is over now. We can leave and head home to Brooklyn. The buildings can be fixed. We can come back in a week or a month and try again to learn about the stock market with Mr. Bauer.

I try to imagine what Grandma Mimi is doing at this moment. Does she know what's happening? Is she worried about me? In my head, I talk to her. I tell her that she's the smartest person I know. I thank her for always being there for me. I let her know how much I appreciate her. And I say that I know how much she loves me, too. I pray that Grandma Mimi is safe.

I can't stop myself from worrying about the people and things I love dearly. My parents, my friends from Queens, even the men who play chess on my old block! I think of all the times they annoyed me. I wish I had appreciated them more. They are a part of my life, and I am not ready to give them up. I would give anything to be back on my old block, with my old friends, right now.

REALITY CHECK:

Did the building really sway when the plane hit it?

Yes, the impact from the plane hitting the South Tower did cause it to teeter. This was not unusual, however. The Twin Towers were built to allow the top floors to sway up to twelve inches. In fact, all skyscrapers are built to bend in strong winds in order to withstand them. From inside the building, you're not supposed to be able to feel it. But even before 9/11, people said they could feel the Twin Towers occasionally sway during very bad storms.

Constructing a skyscraper to move with the wind is what prevents it from crumbling. By allowing a structure to be flexible, it can move without breaking. Tall buildings may look very sturdy, but the taller a building, the more need it has to be able to bend. This is because the wind gets stronger the higher up you go. You might feel a gentle breeze on the ground, but as you go higher, the wind will be much more forceful.

CHAPTER 11

TONY

September 11, 2001, 9:07 AM

The blast throws me. I'm airborne for a split second before I hit the wall. I bang my elbow and land with a thud on the stairs. My dad helps me up and that's when the pain hits. A sharp, stabbing pang radiates down my arm. It's unbearable for a moment before it starts to fade a little to a dull ache.

People pick themselves up and try to continue down the stairs. I wish I could grab my dad and run the rest of the way, but there are too many people blocking us.

Worried there will be another blast, I stay close to my dad. Something wet is raining down from cracks in the ceiling. It has a strong smell that makes my eyes water. I rub my wet hands together. They've become slippery. "What is this?" I wonder aloud.

My dad pauses before answering. "I remember this smell from my summers working the luggage at LaGuardia Airport. It's jet fuel."

I don't understand what my dad is saying. How can it be the gas that planes need to fly? But I don't have time to ask because someone is crying out loudly from behind us.

"Please make space!" they yell. My dad and I move to the right to give them room. A young woman has her arm around an older man's waist. He is holding what looks like a rumpled T-shirt against his head. I can see blood on the side of his face. As they pass, I overhear her saying, "It's going to be okay. I'm going to get you out."

With every passing floor, new people stumble into the stairwell trying to get out of the building. The farther down we get, the slower we are able to go. It is getting hotter. The smoke is getting thicker, too. Everyone stops to make room for a woman in a wheelchair being carried down.

Groups of firefighters squeeze by on their way up. They got here so fast! They are carrying heavy packs. They must be exhausted from climbing so many stairs, but their faces don't show it. They don't even seem scared. They're fearless, willing to risk their own lives to save others.

I have lost track of what floor we are passing. I can barely see through the white smoke. I keep one hand on the wall to steady myself. My dad tries to distract me with a stream of chatter. "Hey, I was thinking. We're overdue for a vacation. Where should we go?" he asks.

I perk up. "Anywhere?" I ask.

"Sure, anywhere," my dad answers.

"Hawaii" is my answer. "Or London! No, wait. Paris! Can we go to the French Open?"

Before he can answer, a woman behind us loses her

footing and cries out as she falls. She bumps right into me as she goes down. I stop to help her up and I notice her face is as red as a tomato. She is trying to get up, but doesn't seem to have the strength to.

I ask Dad to help me. We each grasp beneath an arm and pull her up so she's standing. "Are you alright?" I ask.

She is having a hard time answering. Her eyes are unfocused and her breathing isn't steady. We are just outside the doors to the forty-fourth floor. My dad knows this is one of the "sky lobby" floors. People come to this floor to transfer from a local to an express elevator. "Here," he says. "Let's just get out and take a breather."

The three of us exit the stairwell onto the forty-fourth floor. There is more room here. The air is clearer. Dad tries to keep her calm by introducing us. "We are going to stay with you," he assures her.

After a few minutes, the woman's breathing returns to normal. "Okay, I feel a lot better," she says. "I think I just panicked. I'm sorry."

I understand. It is a day unlike any day I have ever experienced. Panicking seems like a perfectly normal response.

We take the door back to the stairwell we had been in before. We continue the slow walk down. I wonder about my classmates. I know they must be just a few floors down, but it feels like I have lost them.

It is too warm in the stairwell. People are taking off their jackets and throwing them to the side. We step over piles of high heels that have been kicked off. We are getting closer to the ground, but it is getting harder to walk. The lights are off in one section of the stairwell. The air is smoky. Someone calls out instructions: "Grab the shoulder of the person in front of you! If something blocks your way, call out." We continue that way until we reach a part of the stairwell that has working lights.

My dad and I finally reach the tenth floor. We are so close to the ground! But we are moving slower than ever. The smoke is so bad, and it's getting worse. This doesn't seem right. We thought the blast came from above, but what if it was from below? Are we walking closer to danger rather than escaping it?

We have no time to think about it. A girl's voice is calling out to us from the landing below. It's Elizabeth! "Tony! Mr. Bauer! Please help!" she cries.

We squeeze by the few people between us. Elizabeth is kneeling next to Rick. He wheezes with every breath in and out. He is breathing so hard, but can't seem to catch his breath.

"He has asthma," Elizabeth explains. "He's been having a hard time breathing, but it's gotten a lot worse the last few flights."

"Your inhaler," I say. "Where is it?"

Rick shakes his head. He points up.

Elizabeth looks worried. "Listen to me," she says. "He needs help, now. Mr. Bauer, can you carry him down? It's the fastest way to get him to safety."

Dad looks at me, then Elizabeth. "You two have to stay together. Keep taking these stairs down to the lobby. No matter what. Stick together."

We both nod our heads. "Promise me," he says.

"I promise," we both reply.

Dad picks Rick up like a baby. He leans down to me to whisper, "I love you." And with that, he is off. We can hear him calling for people to make room to get by. We try to follow as closely as we can, but Dad is too fast and the space he makes gets swallowed up quickly. Soon, I can't even see him anymore. In fact, now I don't see anyone else I know.

In a crowd of people all trying to escape, Elizabeth and I only have each other.

REALITY CHECK:

How did people with physical impairments get down to safety?

Unfortunately, many people with physical disabilities died that day. We know of at least two people in wheelchairs that were carried down stairwells to safety by kind strangers. However, many more people with mobility challenges died waiting for help to arrive.

After the attack, experts examined what could have been done differently. How could more lives have been saved? Many workers in the World Trade Center who couldn't walk the stairs had been given evacuation chairs. These special chairs are very light. They allow wheelchair users to be more easily carried down to safety in an emergency. But there was not enough training in how to use these chairs. Without a clear plan, the evacuation chairs were useless.

People were simply not prepared for the events of 9/11, and this resulted in the loss of many lives. We now know that it's not enough to have the proper equipment. People must also be trained in how to use that equipment.

CHAPTER 12

ELIZABETH

September 11, 2001, 9:55 AM

As promised, Tony and I stick close together after Mr. Bauer leaves with Rick. As we walk, I don't say much. I feel exhausted in a way I have never felt before. My feet are sore. I am damp with sweat. It feels like I am coated in a fine layer of filth.

More than that though, my brain feels tired. I haven't had a moment of calm since that first *BOOM!* in the conference room. I feel like I could fall asleep right here in this stairwell.

I stumble over a briefcase and Tony motions for me to put my hands on his shoulders. This helps me feel more steady on my achy feet.

My spirits pick up as we get closer to the bottom. As we walk down the last few flights, we can feel the relief in the air. But as excited as I am to get out of this building, I think about the people who may not have made it out yet.

I follow Tony out into the lobby. "We made it," I say with a sigh. But that thought is quickly replaced with confusion. This isn't the lobby. This is a construction zone.

We must have made a wrong turn. As far as I can see, everything is a dusty gray. The windows are blown out. Broken glass, wires, and bits of metal cover the floor. Smoke and dust hang in the air.

I don't recognize this place. How can it be that it was so shiny and grand just a few hours earlier?

A firefighter directs us to the exit, which is just below us. I look to the doors where we had entered. Rubble is falling, crashing into the ground from above. The ground is covered in debris.

In a daze, we make our way outside to Church Street.

The streets are blanketed with emergency vehicles. There is no sign of our class or Mr. Bauer.

I turn to Tony. "What do we do now?"

As if answering my question, a roar like a speeding train blares around us. Someone yells "RUN!" We take off as fast as we can down the street. The rumbling continues as a cloud of dust rushes toward us from behind, hitting our backs with tiny bits of the wreckage. It is all around us, making it hard to breathe. I pull my shirt up over my mouth to try to block inhaling all of this poison air.

Tony stumbles and falls to the ground, hard. I reach back and pull him up. He's limping, and it looks like he's skinned his palms on the rough concrete. We have no time to stop, though.

I spot an office building with revolving glass doors. I grab Tony's hand and pull him through the doors and into the lobby with me. Outside, the dust cloud rushes by. From the inside of the glass, all we see is solid white.

We sputter and cough the ash out of our mouths.

We wait there until the fog starts to clear. When we step back out into the street, everything is covered in a layer of chalky dust. I am amazed. It looks like we have traveled back in time. We are old-timey actors in an old black-and-white movie.

I wipe my hands on the front of my jeans. I am about to tell Tony that he looks like a gray-haired old man. But something in his expression alarms me. Tony is frozen. His eyes, unblinking, stare back in the direction we had just run from. I turn to see what's wrong. There is only one building standing where the Twin Towers used to be. The South Tower, the one we just escaped, has collapsed.

REALITY CHECK:

WHY DID THE TOWERS FALL?

The Twin Towers were actually built to withstand being hit by a plane. When designing it, the engineers kept in mind a 1945 plane crash that happened at the Empire State Building. At the time, the Empire State Building was the tallest building in the world. Due to thick fog, the pilot of a military aircraft, a B-25 Mitchell bomber, couldn't see the top of the building and struck it. When it crashed, the three members of the flight crew, along with eleven civilians, died. Thankfully, the building didn't collapse.

So at the time of their construction, when the Twin Towers were to be the new tallest buildings in the world, the events of 1945 were kept in mind when fashioning what many believed to be among the strongest skyscrapers in existence.

There is some debate about why exactly the towers came down. One thing experts agree on is that the large amount of highly flammable jet fuel played a part. It caused the fires to burn at a very high temperature. This excessive temperature weakened the steel columns. It is also thought that the planes knocked out the buildings' water supply on impact. Without water, the sprinklers didn't work, so the fires raged out of control.

An investigation after 9/11 led to changes in the way skyscrapers are built, making them safer. New buildings have sprinkler systems that cannot be knocked out. Many high-rises are also built with wider stairwells. Some even have a separate stairwell just for firefighters.

CHAPTER 13

TONY

September 11, 2001, 10:05 AM

I can't believe what I am seeing. The building my dad worked in all these years is gone. The same building I visited so many times. The same building I *was just inside of*!

In its place is a smoking pile of rubble. The North Tower is still standing, but it is hard to see the top part of it through the smoke and flames. Will that building come tumbling down, too?

Across the street, someone calls out my name. It is hard to recognize anyone. Everyone is covered in ash. But I know the voice. Jake!

Elizabeth and I run over. Jake is standing with Asim and Chloe P! I am so happy to see familiar faces.

"You guys okay?" I ask. My palms hurt, and I'm bleeding a little bit. I wipe them on my pants, and try not to think about the sting.

"Yeah, I think so," Jake replies.

"Do you know if everyone got out?"

The boys shake their heads. "We got separated from everyone in the stairwell," Chloe explains. "More and more people kept coming through. It was impossible to stay together."

A police officer is coming down the block, yelling for everyone to walk north. "It's not safe here! You must walk up to Canal Street. Let's go!"

Jake, Asim, and Chloe start to walk, but I don't budge. "Guys, I can't leave. I need to find my dad."

My friends look at each other. Asim speaks first, "I hear you. I totally get it. But it's not safe here. You heard what they said."

I can't leave without my dad. I need to know that he

is okay. "You guys go," I say to the group. "I need to go back. I need to find my dad."

"Are you sure?" Jake asks.

"Yes," I say. "Stay together. If you see my dad, tell him I'm looking for him."

They start to walk away, but Elizabeth stays put. "You coming?" Jake asks her.

Elizabeth pauses. She shakes her head no. "I'm going to stay with Tony. I promised I would."

I nod, a small gesture of thanks. But inside, I feel really happy. I don't want to be by myself. Not now. Not here.

REALITY CHECK:

WHERE DID THE NAME GROUND ZERO COME FROM?

The term "ground zero" was coined long before 9/11. It was originally used to describe the area where a bomb had exploded. Later, it was used as a term for a place that experienced a violent change.

In 1993, after the bombing of the World Trade Center, the site was first called Ground Zero. Eight years later, after 9/11, it was given that name again. It took so long to rebuild the site that the name stuck. People still refer to it as Ground Zero, even though it is now the site of a shiny new complex.

CHAPTER 14

ELIZABETH

September 11, 2001, 10:10 AM

I am worried about Tony. Since we ran into his friends, he seems to be getting more and more concerned. He wants to find his dad so badly. But the area around the World Trade Center is a complete disaster zone. Hundreds of people are running around on the street, trying to figure out where to go. Police officers yell, "Keep it moving!"

We walk down the block calling for Tony's dad.

"Stephen Bauer!" we shout. Over and over again until our throats are sore.

I find a short set of stairs leading to an official-looking building. I stand tiptoe at the top and turn to look in every which way for Mr. Bauer. But there are so many people. It is no use.

Tony's mood darkens. I try to keep things light by asking him questions.

"Hey, if you could only eat one food for the rest of your life, what would it be?" I ask.

"Burgers," he says.

"Would you rather kiss a snail or hug an armadillo?"

"Armadillo, definitely."

Tony's sticking to one-word answers. Just when I think there's no way to get through to him, he has a question for me. "Do you think he made it out?"

I stop and grab his arm. "Yes!" I say. "He was in front of us, remember? He would have gotten out way before us."

"I know, but . . ." he trails off.

I can't really imagine how he is feeling at this moment. I want to fix it, but I know I can't. We walk in silence for a minute. I notice a line forming at a pay phone and have an idea.

"Wait! Does your dad have a cell phone?" I blurt out.

Tony's face lights up. "Yes!" He thinks for a second. "But I don't have any money. Do you?"

I don't have any change on me. But I do have the five-dollar bill Grandma Mimi gave me! I point to a deli across the street. Maybe we can get change there.

When we enter, a bell on the door jingles. I expect it to be crowded or somehow stranger than normal. But it looks totally like it should, just like every other deli. There are racks of every flavor of potato chip. The walls are lined with refrigerated cases filled with sodas, juices, and other drinks. By the cashier, there is a display of scratch-off lottery tickets. I imagine on a typical day, people come in here to get sandwiches and coffee.

The cashier looks surprised to see us. "Can I help you?" he asks.

"Actually, yes," I say. "Could you please give us change for the pay phone?" I slide the bill across the counter.

He blinks. "Are you two by yourselves?" he asks.

Tony answers first. "We are. We need to find my dad. Do you have quarters?"

The man shakes his head. His eyes are sad and soft. "You must be terrified out here by yourselves. Here, I have a phone." With that, he hands Tony a cordless phone.

While Tony dials, I grab two waters from the beverage case. Before even paying, I chug half of one. The cold water feels amazing on my dry throat.

Walking back to the counter, I can hear Tony on a call. "Dad!" he says. "Yes! . . . Yes, we're okay. . . . I am, yeah. She's right here."

I place the bottles on the counter next to my money. The man slides the bill back toward me. "Hold onto it," he says. "In case you need it later." I smile and thank him.

Tony has finished up his call. He tells me, "We're going to meet my dad on the corner of Church and Barclay Streets."

He turns to the clerk. "Thank you for your kindness. It means a lot."

"It's my pleasure," he replies. "Be safe!"

With newfound energy, we head back out into the street. We walk alongside hundreds of stunned New Yorkers to find Tony's dad.

As we walk, I think about my family. With all the excitement, I'd forgotten to try to call them. I imagine Mom and Grandma Mimi in the kitchen, watching the news on the small TV on the counter. I want so badly to let them know I am alright.

REALITY CHECK:

WHY DON'T ELIZABETH AND TONY HAVE CELL PHONES?

In 2001, it would have been very uncommon for a sixth grader to have a cell phone. Around this time, most adults in New York City carried a mobile phone, but they were much different than today's phones. They didn't have the internet or the ability to give you directions. They didn't tell you the weather. They couldn't even take pictures.

Cell phones from this era made phone calls and sent simple text messages. They didn't have keyboards. Instead of pressing letters to form words, you had to press the number buttons. Every letter could be spelled out by pressing a numeral a certain number of times. It took a long time to type anything out. There weren't even emojis yet!

CHAPTER 15

TONY

September 11, 2001, 10:28 AM

We're walking quickly trying to find my dad. The streets are filthy with dust and ash. Cars are covered in a fine gray powder. We walk alongside people who are crying. Other people stare blankly ahead, like this day has sucked all the feeling out of them. Sirens blare from fire trucks headed to help and ambulances carrying people away to hospitals.

I spot my dad first. He is standing on a corner, watching the street like a hawk. We run the last few yards and my dad wraps me up in a hug. "I was so worried," he tells us. "I just spoke to Ms. Monroe. She's pretty shaken up. But she said everyone is accounted for."

"Rick's okay?" I ask.

"Oh, yes. He's good now. He was able to get to a medic right away. He needed medicine for his asthma, but he got better quickly. His mom works nearby. She came to pick him up."

Dad hands Elizabeth his cell phone to call home. The call won't go through at first. The lines must be jammed. It takes a few tries, but she finally gets her mom. "Mommy," she cries. "I'm okay, I'm alright."

While Elizabeth is on the phone, my dad and I step off to the side. "When the tower collapsed and then we couldn't find you . . . I just . . ." My eyes get red.

Dad pulls me in tight again for another hug. I breathe in the woodsy smell of his aftershave. I feel my pulse slow down. "I know how you felt. I was terrified, too," he tells me. He smooths down the hair on the back of my head.

Elizabeth wipes away tears as she finishes her call.

"My mom said to stay with you guys. And she wanted me to say thank you."

My dad smiles. "Of course. Now, let's get going. The train is this way."

We walk a block to the subway. A police officer is standing by the entrance. "Keep it moving!" he announces. "We need to clear the area. Please keep walking north."

Dad gets the officer's attention. "Excuse me, can you tell me how to get to Brooklyn?"

The officer responds loudly for everyone to hear. "I'm very sorry, I have no information on the trains. Right now, we are clearing the entire area! Please keep walking north!"

We pause to figure out what to do next. I try not to think about the awful smell, but it is hard to ignore. It isn't like any smell I have ever experienced. Burnt metal mixed with melted plastic and singed paper. I don't want to think about what else it could be. It lingers in the air with the smoke and dust.

Helicopters pass overhead and sirens wail. A familiar sound growls from downtown. Terrified, I turn to look. My eyes go wide and I gasp. Starting at the top of the building, we watch the North Tower collapse in slow motion. Floor by floor, it looks like the building is sinking into the ground. Tons of debris rain down on Lower Manhattan. The roar gets louder as it hits the ground. Another thick cloud plunges to the street and spreads outward. I turn and yell, "Run!"

REALITY CHECK:

WHAT WERE SOME OF THE OBJECTS FROM THE TOWERS THAT WERE LATER FOUND?

In the months and years after the attacks, thousands of items from the World Trade Center were recovered. From handwritten notes to jewelry to pieces of the buildings, each one tells an important story.

All the way over in Brooklyn, people found pieces of burned paper that traveled across the East River. Carried three miles by the wind, a man found a Peace Corps application on his car's windshield.

Items were found all over Lower Manhattan. Most were discovered in the days and weeks after the attacks. A few things weren't found until quite a bit later. In 2013, a piece of a plane wing was found a few blocks from the site. It had been stuck in a thin, unused space between buildings for twelve years.

More than 10,000 of these items are on display at the 9/11 Museum.

CHAPTER 16

ELIZABETH

September 11, 2001, 11:00 AM

My lungs are burning as I'm running, again, from a cloud of dust. My eyes are stinging and it's really hard for me to see anything. I ignore the soreness in my legs and force them to keep going. I hear someone shout, "Oh, no!" again and again. The other tower has fallen.

We duck inside a small doorway. Mr. Bauer tells us to cover our mouths and noses with our shirts. It makes it easier to breathe that way. After a few minutes, the cloud passes. The dust lightens. It seems safe to walk. We head back to the street to find our way home.

All around us, people are sharing information as they walk. The subways and buses aren't running.

Manhattan is closed to all incoming and outgoing traffic. All of Lower Manhattan is being evacuated.

Mr. Bauer begins talking to a man walking by himself. Dust-colored and tired-looking, he tells us his story of escape from the 105th floor of the South Tower.

"I was in a meeting when the first plane hit. I saw it lodged in a giant hole in the side of the building. The flames looked red-hot. I knew right away we had to get out of that building," he tells us. "We started down the stairs. But then came the announcement that it was safe to stay in the building. I begged them not to go back. They thought I was being silly. I made it down to the seventy-second floor by myself when I felt the second plane hit right above me," he says.

It takes me a moment to understand what he has just said. *The second plane.* With all that happened that morning, I didn't know for sure what caused it. I knew it was bad. I knew people were injured. And that others probably lost their lives. But I was still holding out hope that it was all a terrible accident. I don't hear the rest of the story before the man goes left, continuing on his way uptown.

I am lost in thought as we head to the Brooklyn Bridge. I am tired and we have a long way to go. Surrounded by people, yet feeling so alone, I start to cry.

Tony and his dad don't notice at first. But as we approach the bridge, my sobs get louder.

When they see how upset I am, they stop. Tony puts a hand on my shoulder. "Are you alright?" He asks.

"I don't . . . I don't know," I say. "I don't think we should be on a bridge. What if it's not safe?"

Mr. Bauer pauses. He doesn't know what to say. Is he worried about the bridge, too?

He replies carefully. "I understand what you're saying, Elizabeth," he starts. "You're not wrong to be scared. I'm scared, too. What happened today was awful. But this is the only way to get home."

I feel woozy. I am breathing very fast.

"Let me teach you something my mom taught me. Close your eyes," he tells me. "Take a deep breath in while counting to three. I'll do it with you. One, two, three."

Together, we breathe in.

"Now, we'll breathe out to the count of four. One, two, three, four."

Together, we exhale.

We do it a few more times until we feel calmer. I open my eyes and look out at the crowd pouring onto the bridge. Hundreds of people are walking together. People of all different ages and backgrounds, they're all side by side. On an ordinary day, we might not even really see one another. But now we are united by the terrible things we all saw and felt today.

"Okay," I say. "I'm ready."

REALITY CHECK:

WITH ALL PUBLIC TRANSPORTATION HALTED,
HOW DID PEOPLE GET HOME THAT DAY?

Thousands of people walked across bridges to get home to the outer boroughs. The Brooklyn Bridge, Williamsburg Bridge, and Manhattan Bridge carried people from Lower Manhattan to Brooklyn.

If you lived in New Jersey, Queens, or Brooklyn, you might have waited hours for a boat. Regular ferry service was stopped, but special ferries and a good deal of watercraft that was commandeered by local authorities were used to help get people off the island.

The subways were out of service for hours. By the afternoon, a few trains were back up and running. But some stations in Lower Manhattan were so badly damaged that they didn't reopen for years.

Many people couldn't even make it home on 9/11. They stayed with family, friends, or acquaintances in hotels, or anywhere they could find.

CHAPTER 17

TONY

September 11, 2001, 1:30 PM

The long walk home takes two and a half hours. By the end, my feet are screaming at me. The pain in my arm has thankfully been reduced to a dull ache. I'm sweaty, dirty, and hungry.

On the bridge, someone had a radio. We learned more about the sad events of the day. Not only did two planes crash into the Twin Towers, but two other planes were hijacked as well. One crashed into the Pentagon, in Washington, DC. The other ended up in a field in Pennsylvania. We don't yet know for sure, but it sounds like brave passengers took that plane down to prevent a bigger tragedy.

I look out over the water at the burning piles that used to be the World Trade Center. I know this is a day I will remember forever. The sights, sounds, and smells will stick with me for the rest of my life.

When we drop Elizabeth off at her apartment, her grandma is waiting outside with cookies for us. She wraps her granddaughter in a long hug. It feels strange to leave Elizabeth. In just a few hours, we have been through so much together. I give her a hug. "See you in school!" I say as we say goodbye.

I turn to leave, but Elizabeth calls out, "Wait!"

"Can I email you?" she asks. I smile with relief. We haven't known each other long, but she feels like a friend now.

Ever since I learned that the attacks were carefully planned, I have wondered why anyone would want to hurt so many innocent people.

My dad tries to explain it as best as he can. "There are people around the world that hate the United States," he says. "And they are prepared to do anything to hurt this country and send a message."

I try to understand. "But the hijackers. They died, too," I say.

"They did, yes. I know it might not make sense, but the hijackers were convinced that they were sacrificing their lives for a good cause."

"A *good cause?*" I am shocked. How could killing thousands of people ever be for a good cause?

Dad sighs. "I don't know, Tony. I know it's hard to follow. The world can be a confusing place sometimes. The US tries to help countries around the world gain freedom and democracy. But sometimes it doesn't work very well, and sometimes the US even makes mistakes. And there are those who think the US should mind its own business. Not everyone believes in our idea of freedom. And some think that violence is the best way to have their ideas heard."

I still don't understand why anyone would want to hurt innocent people. And I don't think it will ever make sense to me.

REALITY CHECK:

*WHAT HAPPENED TO THE TWO
OTHER PLANES THAT WERE HIJACKED?*

On the morning of 9/11, American Airlines Flight 77 took off from Washington, DC. It was headed to California. About thirty-five minutes into the flight, five hijackers took over and steered the plane south toward the Pentagon. They hoped to destroy the building that was seen as the heart of the US military.

The plane crashed into the western part of the building. All sixty-four people on the plane, including the hijackers, died in the crash. Inside the building, 125 people lost their lives.

The fourth plane to be hijacked that day was United Airlines Flight 93. It left Newark, NJ, on the way across the country to California. After forty-six minutes, the hijacked plane turned and also headed to Washington, DC. Passengers, aware of the earlier three plane attacks, tried to take back the plane to stop the hijackers from carrying out their plan. The plane ended up going down in a field in Shanksville, Pennsylvania. All forty-four passengers, including the four hijackers, died.

CHAPTER 18

ELIZABETH

September 17, 2001, 7:45 AM

School is cancelled for the rest of the week. I spend most of the time watching the news with my family and doing a crossword puzzle with Grandma Mimi. I call Phoebe, Rosie, and Ella. I tell them all about escaping the World Trade Center. I describe a day that will be with me for the rest of my life.

The principal of my new school calls to check in. She lets us know there will be an assembly when we're back in school. Our class will also have a counselor available to help anyone who feels sad or scared about 9/11.

Tony and I email back and forth. At first, we just talk about escaping the World Trade Center. But slowly we start to talk about other things. Turns out we have a lot in common. We're both only children. We both love the Simpsons. We're even reading the same book!

When we go back to school the following Monday, we all have so much to catch up on.

I am standing outside the building with Tony and Jake when Ayelet and Rick walk up. I am quiet for a moment. But as soon as we start talking about last Tuesday, I open up.

We all describe the best and worst things we saw that day. We have all experienced sorrow, fear, and confusion. But there are also so many stories of bravery, kindness, and generosity, too. Ayelet remembers a woman handing out water to people on the street. Jake talks about the firefighters running *toward* the towers as they collapsed. And as much as our stories are similar, we each experienced the day so differently.

Over the weekend, my family and I walked to the Brooklyn waterfront to see across to Lower Manhattan. Days later, there was still smoke rising from the ashes.

Thankfully, the terrible smell was almost gone from the air.

As we walk into the building to start first period, Tony and I make a plan to walk home together after school. We'll invite Asim, Rick, Ayelet, and Chloe P. We can get ice pops. Tony knows of a place where they sell them for a quarter.

I take a seat in class. Ms. Monroe lets us know we will be taking a break from our stock market study. Instead, she wants each student to write about what being a New Yorker and an American means to us. I have so many ideas, I don't know where to begin. Then I think about our escape from the tower. I started that day not really knowing anyone in class. I didn't have any friends as I was the new kid in class. But when the planes hit, all I saw was kindness and unselfishness. Tony and his father helped, the man at the deli gave us water and his phone, the police officers and firefighters helped us and kept us safe.

So, I write about these brave people who risked their

own safety to help me. I write about how we all worked together that day—friends, family, and even strangers, to make it home. We worked together to escape.

Even though the terrorists were able to destroy the towers, no one can shake my pride in my city and in my friends and family.

REALITY CHECK:

WHAT WAS BUILT TO REPLACE THE TWIN TOWERS?

It took a long time to decide what to do with the area where the Twin Towers once stood. Families of the victims wanted a memorial. The company that owned the land wanted to build another skyscraper.

In the end, they reached a compromise. Ten years after 9/11, on September 11, 2011, a memorial was revealed to the public. Called Reflecting Absence, it featured two pools built in the space where the North and South Towers once sat. The names of the victims of both the 2001 and 1983 terrorist attacks are etched into the outer walls of the pools so they will be remembered forever.

In 2006, construction started on One World Trade Center. It took over eight years to finish. Standing at over 1,700 feet, it's the tallest building in the western hemisphere.

Visitors to the site can also visit a 9/11 museum, a shopping mall, and a park. There is also a large sculpture called the Oculus. It was built with slats to let in light. It represents the brightness that can come after a dark tragedy.

○ **8:14 AM**—United Airlines Flight 175 takes off from Logan Airport in Boston, Massachusetts. There are 65 people on the flight: 51 passengers, 9 crew members, and 5 hijackers.

○ **8:19 AM**—Another flight from Boston, American Airlines Flight 11, is taken over by hijackers. Two flight attendants, Betty Ong and Madeline Amy Sweeney, contact American Airlines and provide information. The FBI is also informed.

○ **8:20 AM**—Near Washington, DC, American Airlines Flight 77 takes off from Dulles International Airport. There are 64 people on the flight: 53 passengers, 6 crew members, and 5 hijackers.

○ **8:42 AM**—In Newark, New Jersey, United Airlines Flight 93 takes off from Newark International Airport. There are 44 people on board: 33 passengers, 7 crew members and 4 hijackers.

○ **8:46 AM**—The hijackers crash Flight 11 into the World Trade Center's North Tower.

○ **9:03 AM**—The hijackers crash Flight 175 into the South Tower.

○ **9:37 AM**—The hijackers crash Flight 77 into the Pentagon.

○ **9:42 AM**—All flights over and to the continental United States are grounded by the Federal Aviation Administration.

○ **9:59 AM**—The World Trade Center's South Tower collapses.

○ **10:03 AM**—The passengers of Flight 93 heroically try to take control of the plane. The hijackers crash the aircraft in a field in Shanksville, Pennsylvania.

○ **10:28 AM**—The North Tower collapses.

○ **10:57 AM**—Lower Manhattan is ordered to evacuate, and the city asks the National Guard for help.

○ **5:20 PM**—Wreckage from the North Tower damages 7 World Trade Center, causing fires that burn throughout the afternoon. At 5:20 p.m., the building collapses.

Find Out More

9/11 Memorial & Museum: 911memorial.org/learn/resources

Brown, Don. *America Is Under Attack: September 11, 2001: The Day the Towers Fell*. New York: Square Fish, 2014.

Fleck, Jessika. *Molly and the Twin Towers: A 9/11 Survival Story*. Minnesota: Stone Arch Books, 2021.

O'Connor, Jim. *What Were the Twin Towers?* New York: Penguin Workshop, 2016.

Tarshis, Lauren. *I Survived the Attacks of September 11, 2001*. New York: Scholastic, 2012.

Zullo, Allan. *10 True Tales: Heroes of 9/11*. New York: Scholastic, 2015.

Selected Bibliography

Dwyer, Jim and Kevin Flynn. *102 Minutes: The Untold Story of the Fight to Survive Inside the Twin Towers*. New York: Times Books, 2005.

Rinaldi, Tom. *The Red Bandanna*. New York: Penguin Press, 2016.

Wright, Lawrence. *The Looming Tower: Al-Qaeda and the Road to 9/11*. New York: Vintage, 2007.

Look for more books in
the Escape From... series!

ESCAPE FROM ...

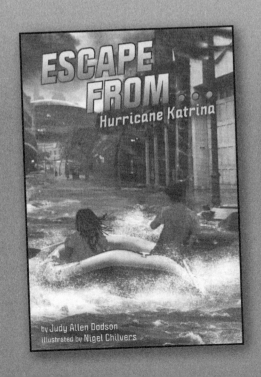

ESCAPE FROM... Pompeii

by Ben Richmond
illustrated by Nigel Chilvers

ESCAPE FROM... the Titanic

by Mary Kay Carson
illustrated by Nigel Chilvers

Read on for a sneak peek
of Escape From . . .
Hurricane Katrina

ESCAPE FROM...
Hurricane Katrina

by Judy Allen Dodson
illustrated by Nigel Chilvers

little bee books

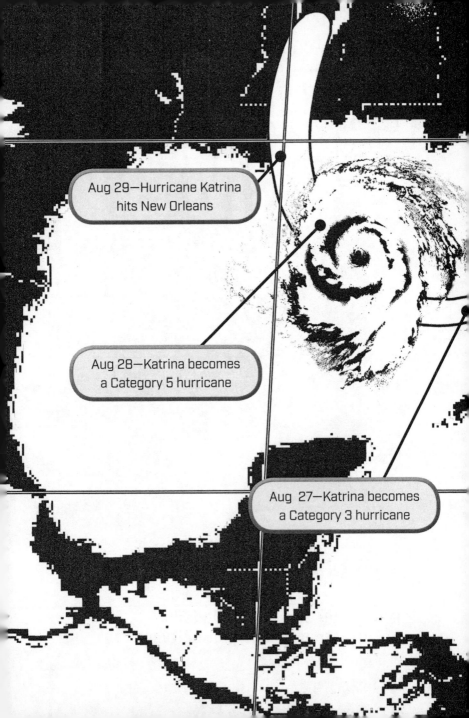

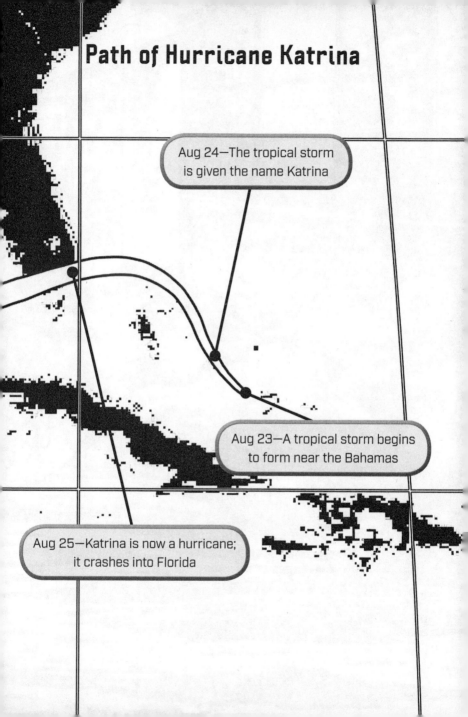

CHAPTER ONE

SOPHIE

Friday, August 26, 2005, 12:00 p.m.

"Swimmers, take your mark. Get set . . ." *BEEP. Splash!*

I dive into the pool, and I can feel my heart pounding in my throat. Even though I'm used to it by now, it's still difficult for me to hold my breath as I take four long strokes underwater. I swallow a gulp of water before coming up for air. I recover, no problem, but I lose valuable time. "Kick, kick, kick!" I chant in my head over and over again with each stroke. My legs slap against the water, heavier and slower than usual, and they don't feel attached to my body. My rhythm is off today. Mama and Daddy aren't here to cheer for me like they have been at my past meets. Mama had to get treatment for her cancer, and Daddy had to stay with her. It feels different without them in the stands.

I'm distracted. "Just swim," I tell myself. "Focus." So what if this is my first sixth-grade swim meet of the season and the girls are bigger and stronger than me? The girl to my right is now ahead of me by a foot, and I panic. I'm losing when I know I can win! Freestyle is my best stroke. I can hear Mama say, "Relax and match your rhythm to Sweet Emma Barrett," as she slaps those piano keys, playing my favorite jazz. Suddenly, my strokes don't feel as choppy and I pick up the pace. My first twenty-five yards are done and I do my flip turn. I've got this. Now I can hear Daddy *tap, tap, tap* tapping his feet to his favorite jazz performer, Charles "Buddy" Bolden. I'm gliding through the water with ease now, my rhythm as smooth and strong as a song. I'm in the flow of the water. Down to the last twenty-five yards, I find my third gear. I take fewer breaths, and cup my hands and pull the water behind me—hard —with each stroke. I sneak a glance to my left, and the girl and I are neck